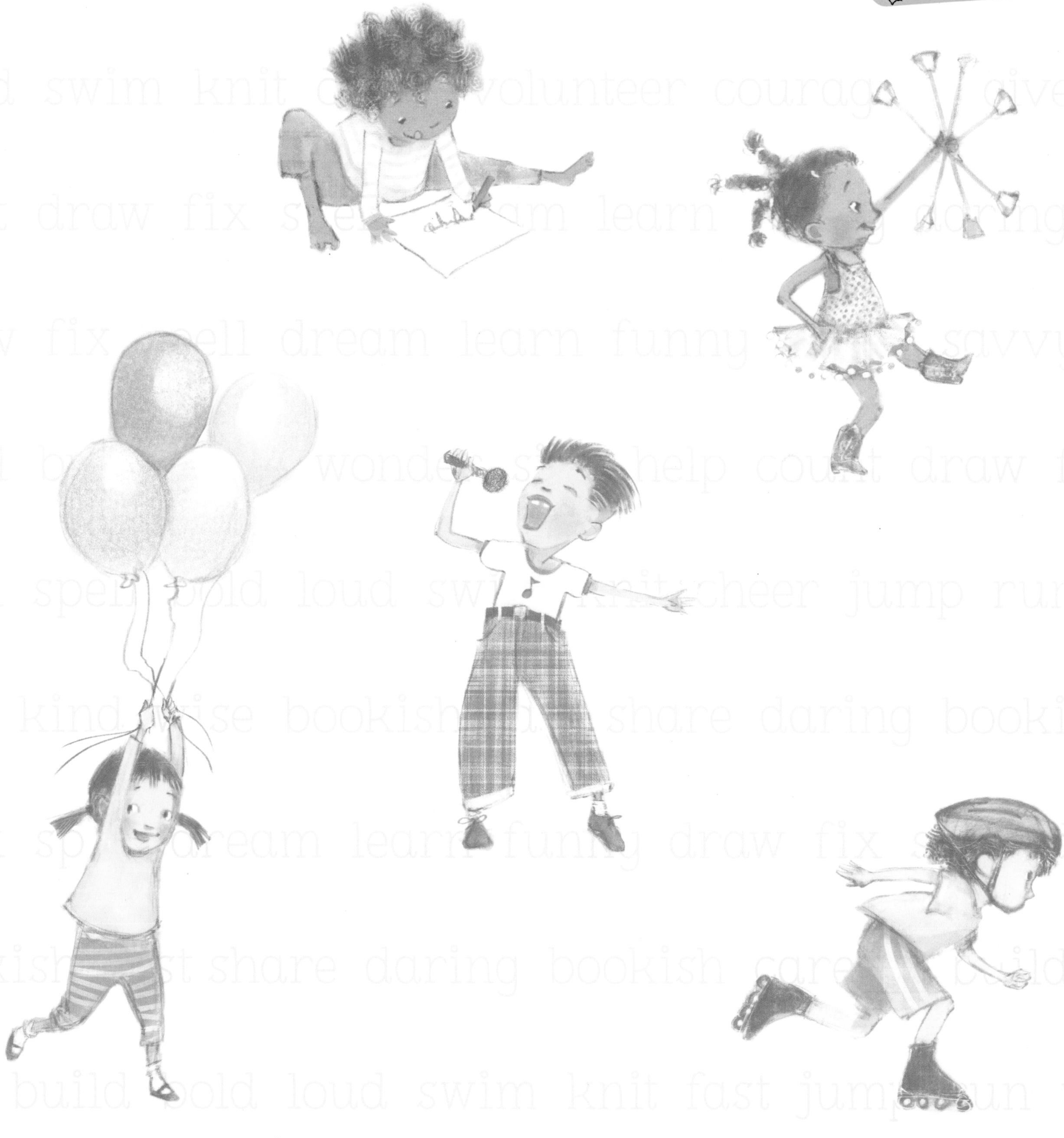

Remarkably
YOU

Remarkably YOU

Written by Pat Zietlow Miller

Illustrated by Patrice Barton

HARPER

An Imprint of HarperCollinsPublishers

Remarkably You

Text copyright © 2019 by Pat Zietlow Miller

Illustrations copyright © 2019 by Patrice Barton

All rights reserved. Manufactured in China.

ISBN 978-0-06-242758-8

Typography by Rachel Zegar
The artist used pencil sketches and mixed media, assembled and
painted digitally, to create the artwork for this book.

18   19   20   21   22   SCP   10   9   8   7   6   5   4   3   2   1

❖

First Edition

To two remarkable people—Daniel Wells and Riley Wells
—P.Z.M.

For my remarkable godson, Colin, with love
—P.B.

You might be bold.

You might be loud.

Leading parades. Drawing a crowd.

You might be timid.

You might be shy.

Quietly watching your neighbors go by.

You might be small,

one tiny sprout.

Learning new things when you're out and about.

You might be big,

practically grown.

Coming and going with friends of your own.

No matter your volume, your age, or your size,

YOU have the power to be a surprise.

You have the know-how.

You're savvy and smart.

You could change the world.

Are you willing to start?

Don't sit on the sidelines.

Be part of the fray.

Go after your passions a little each day.

Find what needs fixing.

Repair what you can.

Then choose a new problem and do it again.

Perhaps you're uncertain. Not sure what to do.

Just look for the moments that let you be you.

Like, maybe you're funny.

Or bookish.

Or fast.

Or maybe you're
always decidedly last.

Perhaps you like counting.

Or drawing all day.

Or finding invisible dragons to slay.

You have your own spirit, unparalleled flair.

So rock what you've got—every day, everywhere.

Perhaps you wander.

Or wonder.

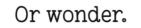

Or sing.

The world needs your voice and the gifts that you bring.

You can make a difference.

In big ways.

Or small.

You won't know how much till you give it your all.

So find what you're good at, what you have to give.

Then go share your sunshine wherever you live.

You might be a helper who's first on the scene.

A speller.

A builder.

A rope-jumping queen.

A swimmer who knits.

A cellist who cheers.

A mutt-loving cat cuddler who volunteers.

You are a blessing,

a promise, a prize.

You're capable, caring, courageous, and wise.

You might go unnoticed
or shine like a star.

But wherever you go and whoever you are . . .

Don't change how you act to be just like the rest.

Believe in yourself and the things you do best.

So whether you're daring or careful or kind,

embrace who you are and the way you're designed.

Dream your own dreams.

Hear your own heart.

You could change the world.

You just have to start.

Follow your path.

Do what you love to do.

Be completely,

uniquely,

remarkably

YOU.

spell wise bookish fast share daring bookish
smart savvy kind wise build bold
draw spell dream learn sing help
fast run wander wonder help count
build knit bookish
spell dream learn smart
count draw fix dream learn smart
wander wonder sing count draw
spell learn funny wise
draw fix spell dream learn daring bookish